Mystery of the

Holiday Hustle

A Mallory Beck

Cozy Holiday Novella

Denise Jaden

MYSTERY OF THE HOLIDAY HUSTLE
First Edition. November, 2020.
ISBN: 9798558494365

Join My Mystery Readers' Newsletter Today!

Sign up now, and you'll get access to a special epilogue to accompany this series—an exclusive bonus for newsletter subscribers. In addition, you'll be the first to hear about new releases and sales, and receive special excerpts and behind-the-scenes bonuses. Sign up at the web address below:

www.denisejaden.com/tips

Mystery of the Holiday Hustle

A short mystery novella, perfect to round out your Mallory Beck Cozy Culinary Collection... or an ideal way to get into the new series that one reader called "a page-turner with loveable characters and unexpected twists and turns."

A secret social media account, a novelist with a hunch, and the sleuth who unravels the mystery...

When newlywed Mallory Beck helps her bestselling-mystery-novelist husband get his sea legs on social media, she's surprised to find *@CooperBeckAuthor* already pumping up his writing and offering a secret new Christmas story to paying subscribers. Is Cooper lying to her about his inexperience and aversion to social media? And if not, where is this

5

imitator getting photos and videos of Cooper that even Mallory has never seen? When she investigates further, and the clues she uncovers hit—quite literally—too close to home, she is determined to get to the truth.

Praise for Denise Jaden's Writing

"A riveting and emotional story."
- The Compulsive Reader

"Losing Faith is a remarkable first novel."
- CM Magazine

"Pitch-perfect portrayals of high school social life."
- School Library Journal

"Highly recommended."
- Library Media Connection

"Harrowing and inspiring."
- Publishers Weekly

TWELVE DAYS BEFORE

Christmas

THE DAY I GOT MARRIED, I thought I would never find a reason to doubt my blissfully-perfect new husband, Cooper. We'd fallen in love almost instantly. He was tall, dark, and hunky, as well as a multi-published bestselling novelist before we'd even left university. He even adored the most unlovable of pets!

This would be our first Christmas as a married couple, our first Christmas sharing a house we could decorate together, and I had a new skip in my step as I hurried up our front walkway, smiling at the twinkle lights surrounding our door and the glimpses of the decorated tree poking through our living room curtains.

I checked the mailbox and sighed when it was empty. I'd spent many an hour retweeting and reposting a social media contest Cooper's favorite author, Albert Rolly, had been holding. Unknown to Cooper, I'd won an advanced signed copy of Albert's upcoming novel *Breathless*. After I'd blathered on to Mr. Rolly about how much Cooper loved his writing and how much I wanted to get the prized book in time for Christmas, he'd gone and sent it without a tracking number. Now all I could do was cross my fingers and hope it wouldn't get delayed with the holiday influx of mail. And check our mailbox daily before Cooper got home.

I sighed again and slid my key into the lock. I didn't have much time. Between my culinary class at the university and my shift at Baby Bistro,

I had just long enough to shower, change, and catch the bus back to campus.

As I waited for the shower to come up to temperature, I clicked on my phone and checked Cooper's Twitter account.

Cooper wasn't much for social media, never had been. He thought all that sort of thing was fleeting and useless, and he had never listened when I suggested that, as a public person of interest, he should at least secure his usernames on all the various platforms. At the urging of his publisher, he finally listened. Of course, by the time he heeded our advice, *@cooperbeck*, *@cooperbeckauthor*, *@cooperbeckmysteryauthor*, as well as *@cooperbeck1-through-189* were all taken.

We had settled on *@cooperbeckwhodunit*. It wasn't ideal, but his publisher suggested if he worked hard, he'd find a following in no time.

That was the thing about my talented husband, though. After a lifetime of most things coming easily to him, he didn't seem to know how to work hard.

Even though I was completing my last year of culinary school, plus cooking five nights a week at Baby Bistro, I did as any doting wife-who-knew-the-social-media-ropes-better-than-her-husband would. I'd gotten his Twitter account warmed up with some tantalizing tweets about his new novel, along with a dozen hashtags.

Besides, I figured if he learned too much about social media too quickly, he might find out about his Christmas gift.

He had five new notifications since I'd gotten in the door.

It was fun—and a little exciting—pretending to be Cooper and conversing with fans online. His Twitter following had quickly ballooned into five digits. On my social media accounts combined, I had a little over three hundred friends and followers, all of whom I knew personally. It took next to no thought to post a pic of a particularly tempting entrée at Baby Bistro or an update about the time and mood of my awakening that day. With my own accounts, there was never any pressure to post something amazing or even interesting. Cooper's interactions often made my face warm as though *I* were the famous person whose very presence online brought a certain buzz and excitement. Each of his posts took more thought, but the need to puzzle out the most buzz-worthy types of posts left me energized.

Tidbits of crime scene research were popular, and because I had been helping as Cooper's research assistant, that fell at least somewhat under my umbrella of knowledge. Photos of our cat, Hunch, were also popular, but those came a lot easier to Cooper—the favored owner of our bristly cat.

I made sure to like or respond to every reply that indicated excitement for an upcoming book release or enjoyment of one of Cooper's already-released novels or short stories. These mindless interactions took up little of my time. Once in a while, there had been a question that required a little more thought.

I ignored the ones that asked, "Are you single?" But today, when I checked in on Cooper's increasingly-busy Twitter account, I saw this message from *@TimothyReads22*: ‹**Is this you too? I already follow you at** *@cooperbeckauthor*›

It made me wonder if there really was another author named Cooper Beck.

When I finished my shower, I was still thinking about the commonality of Cooper's name as I rushed through the living room, said goodbye to Hunch, who was sleeping on the couch and barely spared me one open eye, and headed out the front door. The question kept my attention as I rode the bus toward Baby Bistro. I skimmed Amazon and Goodreads and even LibraryThing, but all I could find was *my* Cooper Beck.

I looked out the bus window. It had snowed again this afternoon, so everything was pretty and white, but it was already getting dark at not even four o'clock. I loved Christmas, but I wasn't a fan of the short daylight hours of winter.

I responded to the tweet to tell *@TimothyReads22*: ‹**This is my official Twitter account. I'm glad you found me!**›

I was already at my stop when my curiosity got the best of me, and I searched "*@cooperbeckauthor*" with one hand, grabbing my bag with the other, and raced off the bus. I hated being late, and I was already cutting it close, but I stopped in place on the sidewalk busy with holiday shoppers when the Twitter account in question loaded onto my phone.

The latest tweet said: ‹**There's a new chapter in my Christmas novel posted! Sign up now to read my new holiday mystery, exclusive to subscribers!**› This was followed by the hashtags *#readitnow, #cooperbeckfans,* and a link that read "*cooperbeckforseriousfansonly.com*".

A second later, a new response popped up from *@TimothyReads 22*: ‹**Great! Interesting new serialized novel, BTW. It's really different!**›

I furrowed my brow toward my phone as a woman knocked into me with her shopping bag and then apologized. Caught up in Cooper's Twitter response, I barely responded. Cooper was working on a novel—he always was—but while I had no idea if it was holiday-themed, his draft was months away from being ready for public eyes. He wouldn't even let *me* read it at this stage. Besides that, there was no way he was out there in the Webiverse tweeting these sorts of things behind my back.

Was there?

But if not my Cooper Beck, who?

His publisher?

But they had specifically asked Cooper to get active on social media. They said that part was his responsibility.

I couldn't make sense of it, but when Corinne, one of Baby Bistro's waitresses, swept by me and said, "Ha, I'm going to beat you for once!" I blinked and remembered the time.

I was officially late.

Corinne arrived late for almost every shift, ready with a different excuse. Her alarm hadn't gone off or she'd lost her phone or her boyfriend forgot to pick her up. Getting to work on time—and more importantly, before Corinne, so as not to end up grouped with her endless list of excuses—was of paramount importance to me.

But she was right. She had beaten me today. I sighed as I swept through the door behind her. Jonas, the manager, quickly adjusted his scowl from being aimed toward Corinne to being aimed toward me. The grimace was a contrast to the peppy holly-jolly Christmas music in the background.

"I'm sorry, I'm sorry!" I said and then clamped my mouth shut before I could blame my lateness on Pennsylvania's unreliable bus system. That would definitely earn me the "Corinne Category" label, which came along with Jonas's constant criticism and scrutinizing. I raced past him toward the kitchen, grabbing an apron from the shelf on my way.

Jonas wasn't the kindest boss in the world. In fact, Baby Bistro had a reputation for staff turnover, mostly because of his cantankerous attitude.

With Corinne's lateness, combined with the way she babbled to anybody and everybody on shift, I was surprised she had lasted three months.

But I needed this job. Chef Paul was willing to give me a reference just as soon as a sous-chef job opening came up at one of the bigger university restaurants.

My hope dwindled for getting out of this misstep unscathed, though, when Jonas followed me to the breakroom, where I quickly discarded my coat, and into the kitchen.

"We don't need lackadaisical loafers around my kitchen, Mallory." His voice boomed right beside my ear. I cringed and wrapped my apron around my waist, and then tried to get away from him, rushing across to the cutting counter. But he followed me, unwilling to let up. "Rory's been here for half an hour, doing your job, I might add."

Jonas motioned across the kitchen to where Rory—a new hire just out of high school with no formal training—stood stirring the soup stock over the stove. Her dark brown ponytail sat high on her head. She wasn't wearing a hairnet *again*—something Chef Paul had admonished her for more than once. I couldn't see her lasting long.

The soup stock wasn't my job, even if the finishing of the soup was, and Rory's shift started earlier than mine, but I bit down on my lip and only nodded. Arguing with Jonas never ended well, especially when he was already in a mood.

"It won't happen again," I said to him, and then I turned on my heel toward the industrial sink to wash my hands.

By the time I returned to the cutting counter, thankfully, Jonas had found something else to bark about in the front of the restaurant. His angry voice echoed through the swing doors, which was my only clue that the dinner rush had yet to arrive.

A good thing, too. Jonas was right—I should have been here earlier, and truth be told, he should pay for me to come in even earlier so the soup had plenty of time to deepen its flavors, but I've never argued that particular point because there was no way I'd make it here any sooner from class.

With one hand, I assembled vegetables that had been plunked onto my counter for dicing, organizing my knives, peelers, and spatulas with the other. As I did this, I read the paper list of specialty menu items taped to the wall in front of me.

I sighed when my eyes settled on the minestrone with swiss chard soup.

Chef Paul was talented, certainly, but not terribly imaginative. I'd made this soup three times last week. The fish special for tonight was a pan-fried tilapia with lemon butter. It would probably be well-seasoned and tasty, and I'd do everything in my power to plate it in a way that would entice surrounding patrons, but I always wished that Baby Bistro would eventually be known for adventurous and memorable dishes, not simply adequately flavorful ones.

Because of my lateness, there was no time to waste, so I prepped the dill sprigs for the fish first and set them aside for later. Then I got busy with tearing the swiss chard and dicing up two types of onion for the soup. Once I had those on the grill and their sweet aroma filled the kitchen, I chopped romaine, cabbage, carrots, and kale for our three regular salads: Caesar, a creamy coleslaw, and kale with apples and walnuts. When Chef Paul was feeling especially motivated, he also offered a special salad of the day. Having not seen our chef yet today, I could tell simply by my list that he wasn't particularly motivated.

I transferred the onion chunks from the grill to the simmering vegetable stock and told Rory, "I can take over now. Why don't you ask Chef Paul what he wants you on next?"

She bounced away, swinging her non-hairnetted ponytail right over the soup as she went.

While slicing up the Honeycrisp apple chunks for the kale salad, I glanced at my simmering soup with a sudden idea. Swiss chard, in my opinion, made the minestrone on the bitter side.

I scooped a little minestrone into a side bowl, added two small apple chunks, gave them a minute to come up to temperature while I finished assembling the kale salad, and then grabbed for a spoon.

One day, I'd be the chef of my own kitchen and I swore, for about the eight-hundredth time, that I wouldn't get complacent.

I leaned back against the metal prep counter and closed my eyes as the flavor of the soup hit my taste buds. The sweet bite of the apple was exactly what the soup needed.

After the one taste test, I wasn't thinking logically. Sometimes this happened to me in culinary classes when I was suddenly overcome and strayed from an assigned recipe. It felt as though it wasn't at all by my own volition. My hands seemed to work independently of my brain.

And an instant later, I had dumped my entire cutting board full of Honeycrisp apple chunks right into the simmering soup.

A sudden loud curse interrupted my train of thought, and I dropped the soup spoon with a clank, right onto the ceramic floor.

Chef Paul.

"What on earth do you think you're doing? There are no apples in my minestrone!"

I swallowed hard. Chef Paul wasn't usually one for accepting other people's ideas. He stood at five-six, barely taller than me, stocky and bald, but bellowed like he was eight feet tall. The reason I'd lasted nearly two years at my job here was because I knew how to humble myself and take direction.

Most of the time, anyway.

"Oh, right," I said, mostly stalling as I tried to decide if it would be better to play stupid or inventive. Or should I offer to quickly strain the apples out before they leaked too much of their *offensive* flavor into his precious soup?

He shook his head. "You're going to have to dump the whole thing and start over. Let's hope the first round of patrons coming in from the cold isn't interested in warming up with soup. Rory!" he yelled. I wondered where she'd disappeared to. Likely vaping in the back alley.

The second Chef Paul found her, he'd have her starting a new pot of stock. I took in a calming breath and decided to jump in with both feet. *Inventive.* "But, I mean, Honeycrisp apples might not be so bad in here."

I reached for a spoon. I knew better than to insubordinately suggest he take a sip. Everyone who worked in the kitchen was regularly grabbing for fresh spoons, loading them with whatever they were cooking at the time, and holding them up to Chef Paul or someone else nearby for a second opinion. I hoped that if I went through the motion, he might take the spoon and stick it into his mouth before he thought better of it.

I babbled on, trying to distract him as I dug the spoon into the brothy soup. "I guess I was busy with the kale salad, you know, and I had to stir the soup. Sometimes when you get busy with more than one thing..." I passed him the full spoon, making sure to include an apple chunk, and held my breath. He slipped it into his mouth.

"I'm really sorry," I babbled on. "And if you think I should start from scratch, I—"

He held up a hand to stop my word deluge. He swished the soup in his mouth. Tilted his head. Finally, a nod.

"It's fine for tonight," he grumbled, and then spun on his heel and headed for the grill.

It wasn't a glowing compliment, but from Chef Paul, being allowed to serve anything that wasn't his specific creation was more than a feat. He moved back and forth from the grill to the side counters where he kept his supplies, agitated energy radiating off him.

"Anything I can do to help?" I asked quietly, more like a subliminal message than an actual question. I had no idea if he was upset by something at the restaurant or maybe it had something to do with his wife or five-year-old son at home.

At first, Chef Paul only grunted, and I figured he either hadn't heard me or didn't think my subliminal message warranted a response, but then he grumbled, "Jonas wants a Christmas menu for next week. I hate Christmas."

I, for one, loved Christmas, but I knew when my boss needed some camaraderie. "I know what you mean. This music is driving me nuts, and we still have almost two weeks to go."

Chef Paul let out something between a huff and a sigh, but his agitated energy was subsiding. I could feel it. All he needed was someone to commiserate with.

"Hey, you know, with those Honeycrisp apples in the minestrone, all you'd have to do is add a little cinnamon, and you could call it a Cinnamon Apple Christmas Minestrone."

Chef Paul furrowed his brow at me and then returned to his julienne bell peppers on the grill. I thought it had been another case of my unstoppable, not to mention unwanted, creative nature taking over, but only a second later, Chef Paul grabbed a small bowl from under the counter, scooped a ladle full of soup into it, and headed for the spice rack.

I watched for a reaction as he added a sprinkle of cinnamon, tasted it, and then added a little more. He grabbed for the sea salt, sprinkled some in, and with his next taste, he nodded.

He didn't come right out and say he liked my idea, but I was beaming for the whole evening after that. The day quickly transitioned from "calm before the storm" to "storm," as it always did on Friday nights. Chef Paul whisked back and forth from the kitchen to the tiny office where he planned his menus and ordered supplies, and he shot even me a half-smile once.

He barked out orders to move this, and cut that, and get the brisket out of the oven, but as the evening passed, it seemed more like he was playing the angry chef than actually being one. When he called out for a kale salad, I had another idea. I quickly plated one and passed that, along with a small bowl of cranberries, over to him.

He looked confused. I tilted my head and raised my eyebrows.

"With a little feta, it could look quite festive," I told him. "Just a thought." With no response, I swung back around and continued about my business, but I hoped I might find my two suggestions on next week's menu.

By the time we had finished with the dinner rush and cleaned the kitchen, I was pooped. I had a text from Cooper and a voicemail from my dad. I'd listen to Dad's message later. His and my sister, Leslie's, messages could sometimes prattle on for fifteen or twenty minutes. Cooper, as usual, was just checking in.

‹How's the night? Anything interesting on the menu?›

I texted back. ‹Maybe. Maybe even one of mine. ☺ How's the writing?›

I did my best not to distract Cooper on my nights off, but he didn't hide the fact that he usually got far more accomplished when my job took me out of the house for the evening.

‹Really! That's great, Mal! I can't wait to hear all about it.›

Tonight, apparently the distractions were someone else's fault.

‹Monia's asking for an updated bio with a little more pizzazz for an interview she's pitching. Pizzazz-on-demand is harder than it sounds. :/›

That actually sounded like something I could help with— although not through texting and certainly not when I was this exhausted. But speaking of Monia, his agent, a sudden thought occurred to me as I dropped my apron into the laundry bin and grabbed for my coat.

‹Hey, Monia hasn't started up a social media account on your behalf, has she?›

The three dots appeared, and I waited him out while he answered.

‹Are you kidding? She doesn't even keep up on her own. It's the one thing we agree on.›

This wasn't exactly true. While Cooper disagreed with Monia about everything from appropriate royalty advances to what books worked best as comparisons to Cooper Beck novels, he generally didn't put up a fuss. I often wondered how Cooper could write such great conflict when in real life he was so conflict-averse.

But if Monia hadn't tweeted about some secret new story, who had?

I could have asked Cooper outright. I probably should have. It wasn't as if I thought he was keeping some big literary secret from me. But maybe a small part of me *did* suspect just that because without much mental process around it, I texted back, ‹**Sorry, gotta go or I'll miss my bus**› and then clicked out of my texting icon.

I said goodbye to Chef Paul and Rory, and even Jonas, before heading out the front door and into the cold midnight air. As I wrapped my scarf tighter around my neck, I headed for the bus stop and pulled up my dad's voicemail message.

As expected, he prattled on for a full fifteen minutes about the leak in his bathroom and how his landlord was trying to get him to pay for it. I shivered as I listened in the cold and waited for my late bus. I continued to listen as I boarded the bus and took a seat.

I didn't really listen to his words, though. I listened to his tone, and his tone, as usual, told me there were many little untruths mixed into his story, all to spin it in his favor.

It didn't matter. It wasn't as though I could talk to his manager and get him out of paying for bathroom repairs, and Dad knew that. Telling stories in which he'd been wronged was just the way he operated.

When his lengthy story finally ended, I navigated away from the phone app, needing something—anything—else to focus on. I opened Twitter and brought up *@CooperBeckAuthor's* account again. His last tweet still directed me to a link with a new secret story.

I had to investigate.

Holding my breath, I clicked the link. Seconds later, a snazzy website with a float-in banner loaded and then faded through several promo photos of Cooper, ones I had seen many times on everything from Amazon to book jackets, but then one I didn't recognize. It captured Cooper laughing and looked like it was outdoors somewhere, maybe at a park or somewhere outside the city. It didn't look like it had been taken by a professional photographer, and I had to wait for the rotation of all the other promo shots before it appeared again so I could study it.

Before it came around again, there was a video clip, this one of Cooper reading animatedly from a book. No sound accompanied the clip, but the background looked like one of the classrooms in the creative writing department. Cooper had shorter hair than I'd ever seen him with, almost a buzz cut to his curly black hair, and so I guessed this was taken before we had met.

I clicked and held my thumb on the screen, hoping it would keep the video playing so I could study it, but instead, it navigated me to a professional-looking sign-in screen. The complicated and flashy website couldn't have been constructed by my Cooper. Certainly not without help, anyway.

A space for a username appeared, followed by one for a password. Underneath that were two buttons: LOGIN and REGISTER.

I couldn't click on the LOGIN option, so I did the only other thing available to me on the page. I clicked REGISTER.

Another flashy page loaded onto my phone. This one didn't include any photos of Cooper, but it did explain more about this strange locked-up website.

Shhhhh...

For serious fans only!

Sign up now for only $9.97 per month and you'll be privy to my new secret serialized novel, not available anywhere else online or in bookstores.

Sign up now and you'll receive a brand new chapter, fresh off my laptop, every single week!

Sign up now! This story will disappear after Christmas. You won't be disappointed!

This was followed by two buttons: one for credit cards and the other for PayPal.

None of it *sounded* like Cooper. If anything, Cooper avoided acting salesy about his writing at all costs. It was one of the reasons he had hesitated to get involved in social media.

I furrowed my brow, but unfortunately, I didn't have another second to think about it. The bus had pulled up against the curb, and I was about to miss my stop.

By the time I got home, Cooper was asleep on the couch with Hunch on his stomach. No doubt, Hunch had been sleeping soundly only moments ago, but with my key in the lock warning him, his ears had pricked up and his tail thumped back and forth against Cooper's legs by the time I got inside.

It was enough to wake Cooper, and for once, I was thankful for that cranky feline. At least I hadn't had to shake Cooper awake because I did need to talk to him.

"Hey, honey," I said, leaning down to give him a kiss. We'd been married for almost six months, dating for a year before that, but the traditional greeting still made me feel like I was playing house, rather than living it.

He smiled up at me, but didn't move to make room on the couch, likely for fear of upsetting his cat's important world. "What time is it?"

I checked my watch and told him. I smelled like cooked grease and sweat, but I didn't care. I sat beside him on the floor. "Hey, listen, I have to ask you something." I pulled out my phone and had the same website loaded within seconds. I hesitated, reminding myself for about the millionth time that Cooper wasn't like my dad and I could trust him not to keep things from me.

I held the screen out to Cooper so he could read it. He blinked a few times, still waking up. He'd left one light on across the room, but it had a yellow glow and lit up the room less than my bright phone screen did.

He blinked a few more times. "I don't get it. Is this something you want to sign up for?"

I furrowed my brow at him. When he handed back my phone, completely unconcerned, I noticed this particular web page didn't mention his name anywhere. No wonder he didn't understand.

I navigated back to the Twitter page so I could show him the whole sequence, but by the time I got there, he had gathered up his blanket and cat and headed for the bedroom. "Can we talk about this in the morning, Mal? I'm beat."

The one good part about this was that he was clearly clueless and didn't recognize the sign-in page. I had a habit of being overly suspicious. It was likely a result of growing up with a shady dad who liked to "spin" things, as he called it. I called it lying. Ever since then, I always unconsciously braced myself for disappointment and betrayal. I rolled my eyes at my stupid suspicions, thinking Cooper could have been running some big network of online sales, without me even knowing about it.

Hunch would have a better chance of doing that.

ELEVEN DAYS BEFORE
Christmas

I DIDN'T SLEEP WELL with the strange Cooper Beck imitator on my mind, but I kept looking over at the real Cooper Beck, sleeping soundly on his back with Hunch curled up into his far side, and knew our conversation about it should probably wait until morning when we were both alert and could figure this out.

I'd known from early on in our relationship that my author-husband had lots of fans, lots of writers who were fans, and even lots of writers who wanted to *be* him. He'd even had an anonymous stalker when we'd first moved into our house, a guy named Rudy Miller, who had been in Cooper's creative writing program. He was on the autism spectrum and didn't have much in the way of boundaries or self-imposed limits. He had followed Cooper around and often imitated his work at school, but the final straw had been when he'd found out where we lived and creepily dropped off a kitchen item he could have only known we needed by studying us through the windows.

After the fact, I'd convinced myself that he had probably been harmless, but apparently, we hadn't been his only stalking victims, and he had soon after been kicked out of school. I had to wonder if this website could be the work of Rudy Miller again, lurking in the background of our lives. I hadn't met him myself, but I'd heard he was a brilliant young man with an incomparable memory. He could be capable of a legitimate case of identity theft. I shivered at the thought.

I had set my alarm for half an hour earlier than I needed to get up for school. Cooper often had to be at the university earlier than me, and I didn't want to miss him.

Turned out, I was up well before him. I studied the website again, wondering if I should click the REGISTER button.

But Cooper and I had both promised to be careful with our money, at least until the next installment of his advance came in, so we could afford to settle down in a house big enough to raise kids as soon as we were done with school. Even ten dollars seemed like more frivolity than we should splurge on. We'd talked about moving to a quaint little town in West Virginia or maybe a mountain village in Montana.

Besides, wouldn't it tip this guy off to our suspicions, if someone with the last name "Beck" suddenly signed up?

I had just filled the coffee maker in the kitchen when Cooper slogged out of our room and down the hall. I'd already showered, so I had a full fifteen minutes to discuss this identity theft issue with him. I knew once I phrased it like that, once he saw this was real, he'd be just as concerned.

"So as I was saying," I started with, in way of a good morning, "I really think we should look into this Internet scam. I only found this one website in five minutes, but maybe there's more. Maybe the reason you had so much trouble getting a username on all the social media platforms was because there are all sorts of Cooper Becks floating around the Internet, pretending to be you."

Cooper furrowed his brow and pressed past me to get the first of the coffee into his cup as it drained through the filter. I didn't really need caffeine. My veins buzzed with anticipatory energy.

Hunch followed close at Cooper's ankles as he took his coffee and headed for his laptop, which he'd left at the kitchen table last night. My laptop case was a plain silver. In contrast, Cooper's had bright stickers covering his—words like *Booyah!* and *Huzzah!* and one big yellow happy face in the middle. We never mixed our laptops up. He booted his up, wiping his eyes.

I sat across from him. "Here, let me show you." I pulled up the fake *@CooperBeck*'s Twitter account. "Someone is posting secret stories, charging money to read them, and pretending they're yours."

I showed him the tweet and then pulled up the signup website on my phone again. By the time it loaded, Cooper had Hunch on his lap. He pulled my phone closer and said, "Let me see that again."

I did, and seconds later, he looked back and forth between my phone and his laptop, typing something into a new email. Hunch, I could tell, was annoyed at me for taking his master's attention away from him. He kneaded Cooper's lap and tried to pet himself under Cooper's arm as he typed.

"I'll run it by Monia," Cooper said. "See what she thinks. It is kind of strange."

I let out a breath that I felt like I'd been holding all night. I was glad he was taking this seriously.

"Flattering, though," he said, standing with Hunch in his arms. He gave me a kiss on the top of my head and then headed for the shower.

NINE DAYS BEFORE

Christmas

TWO DAYS PASSED, AND I couldn't stop thinking about the social media imitator. Every time I went online to check Cooper's Twitter account, I found myself navigating toward the three accounts I'd discovered that all led back to the one sales link: *@CooperBeckAuthor*, *@CooperBeck*, and *@CooperBeckMysteryAuthor*. Not only that, but a little more investigation had revealed that "Cooper Beck"—the imitation version—was also active on Facebook, Instagram, Snapchat, and TikTok—all with a link to the same signup page.

I'd purposely headed to work a full half hour early to start the soup and let the broth develop. As I stirred it over the large commercial stove, I let my questions reverberate through my mind. Cooper had asked Monia twice, and she'd neglected to answer him both times. I had to do *something* to figure out who this guy was.

I checked the posted menu, and while the Cinnamon Apple Minestrone hadn't been included, there was a mention of a Cranberry Feta Salad at the bottom. I smiled.

With the broth simmering, I moved across the kitchen, away from the food, and pulled out my phone. I navigated to Cooper's profile on Twitter and quickly typed in a new bio:

Warning for all Cooper Beck fans: This is the ONLY official Cooper Beck account. Don't fall for any scammers pretending to be me!

I also sent out a tweet, indicating the same thing. I'd been researching Twitter's terms of service to see if there was anything else I could do, and it seemed the next step would be to apply to get Cooper verified. I'd asked Cooper about doing that, as he would have to send in various pieces of ID and other verifications, but he said we should wait to speak to Monia about it first.

I stirred the broth again and then phoned my sister, Leslie, to ask for her expert advice. Growing up with a secretive father and a mother who had abandoned us without a hint of warning, we both had developed natural skills of reading clues to anything that wasn't on the up-and-up. Sometimes we were both overly suspicious because of this, but it had also kept us from getting swindled more than once.

"How's it going?" she answered like she usually did.

I quickly explained the situation. Leslie, like our dad, could prattle on endlessly over a subject before getting to the point. Maybe it was my subconscious attempt to balance her out, but I tended toward the opposite, speaking concisely.

Her kids were making clattering noises in the background. She shushed them before asking, "So this guy is actually charging money to read a chapter at a time of Cooper's published writing?"

I shook my head, even though she wouldn't be able to see it from our kitchen at Baby Bistro. "It says it's a secret story, not available anywhere else, so unless someone's hacked Cooper's laptop..." I trailed off because I hadn't thought of that until now. What if someone *had* hacked his laptop? What if Rudy Miller had broken into our house or gotten a hold of Cooper's laptop at the university? What if he was planning to release

Cooper's new novel and make money off it before he could get it to his publisher?

"So you think it's a faker—publishing their own writing under Cooper's name?"

My brow furrowed. "I don't know." And I truly didn't.

"Give me the URL," Leslie said, and I heard her typing in the background.

I gave it to her, but I was certain she would find exactly what I had.

She typed. And then typed some more. I paced the kitchen, glad to have the space to myself before the restaurant doors opened.

Finally, she came back on the line. "There! I'll send you my username and password. You and Cooper can check it out, see if it's actually Cooper's writing."

"You signed up?" I asked in awe. Leslie was more of a jump-first-think-

51

later type of girl. And I had never been so thankful. "Really?"

"Check it out with your famous husband and let me know when I can log back on there and cancel," she said. "Listen, Casey's burning his mac and cheese. I gotta go."

She hung up, and a second later, my phone buzzed with a new text. Her username and password.

I held my breath as I typed them into the browser on my phone. I wished I had a laptop, but it would have been silly to bring one to work with me.

Only a second later, a new page loaded with a list of linked chapters. The title at the top read "Murder Near the Dark Fortress." Kind of a bland title, especially for a Christmas story. My Cooper was better at punchier titles like "Hidden Bodies" and "Girl After Dark."

The listed chapters went all the way to eighteen, followed by the promise of one new final installment next week.

I clicked on Chapter One.

It loaded quickly, and I could immediately tell, even in the first sentence—a long-winded description about the mountainous terrain—that this wasn't the creative work of my husband. This was definitely a fake making money off his good name.

My phone alarm buzzed, letting me know my shift was about to start. I stuffed my phone into my apron pocket, put the imposter out of my mind for the moment, and headed for my cutting board.

Cooper was particularly busy with a deadline on his latest novel, which likely meant all of his agent interactions remained focused on that. Earlier today, I'd texted him:

‹Did Monia say anything yet about your Internet stalker?›

The more I thought about it, the more I decided I was underplaying the severity of the situation. Who knew what this fake Cooper Beck Author guy was posting under my husband's name that I hadn't found yet? Cooper had been warned to tread carefully with his bestseller status—one wrong comment online and fans could turn on him on a dime.

Unfortunately, Cooper didn't reply until right in the middle of my busy shift. I slipped into the cooler to grab some romaine and took a quick second to check it. I'd come up with all sorts of ammunition to make him realize he might need to cause a fuss to get Monia to take this seriously, but I didn't have a chance to type any of my bullet points out in response to his simple text of: ‹Nope. **I'll check again.**›

After a busy evening at the bistro with no breaks, I finally checked my phone again on the way to the bus stop. Cooper had texted once more.

‹She says to talk to her at the Christmas party tomorrow night.›

I checked the calendar on my phone, glad I'd remembered to book tomorrow night off work. I'd completely forgotten about the Christmas party Cooper's publisher was throwing in downtown Manhattan.

But it would be the perfect opportunity to ask some professionals what to do about this sneaky imitator of Cooper's.

EIGHT DAYS BEFORE
Christmas

THE NEXT NIGHT, WE were in Cooper's car by five o'clock, after a long day of schoolwork for both of us. It was a two-and-a-half-hour drive into New York City, but as a newly accomplished author, Cooper wasn't about to decline such a swanky invitation.

It was frustrating to have such little time at home together, but at least we had this. As he drove, I told him more about the fake Cooper Beck and the secret novel Leslie had gained us access to.

"It's probably good you didn't sign up under our name, just in case," Cooper said, nodding as he got onto the freeway.

"Right?" I said, in agreement. "I probably would've told Leslie not to do it either, but you know her."

Cooper chuckled. He and my sister were a lot alike, often flying by the seat of their pants through life, and letting other people pick up the pieces behind them. Of course, neither of them saw their similarities.

"Read me some of it," Cooper said, motioning to my phone.

I didn't love reading while in the car, especially reading on my phone, so I set up the text to speech option and we both listened as a robotic voice read, "Chapter One – The Lantern."

I sat back into my seat and listened to the chapter I'd already skimmed on the bus ride home last night. The lengthy and too-flowery descriptive parts that had made me screw up my face actually made Cooper balk out loud.

"Readers actually believe this is my writing?" He shook his head.

The robotic voice continued to read, and I hovered my thumb over the stop button, wondering if I should press it. The more the robot read, and the more Cooper shook his head, the more I wished I hadn't told him about my access to the book. As a new author, of course this must bother him.

I guess I was too busy trying to catalog all of the story's many faults, so it surprised me when Cooper said, mid-way through the third chapter, "The premise actually isn't bad. I wish I'd thought of it."

Leave it to Cooper to somehow find endless positivity, even for someone scamming him.

I screwed up my face again and pressed play, hoping for another boring descriptive piece soon, so I could argue his positivity.

We got through five chapters before Cooper said, "I think I've had enough. How about you?"

I agreed. I'd had enough before we had hit the second paragraph. Maybe Cooper could easily let someone pretend to be him publicly, but after years of a dad who took credit for my lawn mowing and kitchen cleaning and a partner in school who liked to take credit for all my best culinary suggestions, I couldn't stand for it. Our concentration on the story had at least helped pass the time and gotten us closer to the city, though, and as traffic thickened, I played navigator, while Cooper drove to the 2nd Act Nightclub where the party was being hosted.

It took us half an hour to find a parking spot that would cost nearly a month's groceries, but then we strode arm in arm toward the club together. We didn't get a lot of chances to go out on dates, certainly not to Manhattan.

I'd worn a cute black dress with red shoes and a purse to bring a little holiday cheer to the outfit. Cooper had dressed with his usual confidence in a bright red dress shirt that hugged the muscles of his chest and tapered along his abs, coupled with black-and-white checkered pants. I hoped I'd be able to glean a little of his confidence and expand my own wardrobe one day.

We strode through the glass doors of the swanky nightclub and were immediately accosted by the black-and-white zigzag flooring. Suddenly, Cooper's pants weren't the most striking visual in the room. The place had brown leather sofas along the walls, many already occupied, and a bar straight ahead.

I wanted to head for the bar— have a glass of chardonnay in hand before I tried to be sociable with the New York City publishing bigwigs— but we didn't have time for that.

Monia beelined across the zigzag flooring, all teased gray hair and focused attention, and had Cooper's hands in hers only a minute later.

I'd only met his agent, Monia Chapman, once before. She spoke with a loud New Jersey accent and had been in the business since the beginning of time, which was why Cooper ended up signing with her, even though he'd had three other offers for agent representation. Since signing his contract, though, I'd realized Monia's public doggedness seemed to only be for show. More than once, she'd suggested Cooper accept what a publisher had suggested for advance royalties, or editing suggestions, or cover art, and Cooper never wanted to fight with her for a better deal, no matter how much I prodded him.

But she did know the business.

I waited for the greetings to pass. About three hundred words burst forth from her to Cooper in the first thirty seconds—updates from his publisher, items expected for next week, and, finally, what this evening would entail. I tried to follow, but my attention was drawn away by men in expensive suits and the somewhat frumpy-looking middle-aged women everyone seemed to be fawning over. They must be well-known authors, I decided.

It was too bad Cooper's favorite author, Albert Rolly, was with a different publisher. Otherwise, I'd march right up to him and ask him why I still hadn't received Cooper's Christmas present.

Actually, I probably wouldn't. But with only a few more mail delivery days before Christmas, I was feeling pretty desperate.

"Mallory! How nice to see you," Monia finally said. And that, apparently, was all the time she had for me. She turned back to Cooper. "Now I need you to keep up appearances about book four. We're not going to mention that you haven't nailed down the premise..."

She led Cooper across the zigzags, and I trailed behind. I had never completely trusted Monia, and I could only trace it back to comments like this one. She'd say whatever she had to in any situation, or force her clients to say what had to be said, no matter how untrue.

A cocktail waitress was making her way around the room. Monia helped herself to two glasses of champagne and passed them back to us. She didn't take one for herself.

At a nearby empty leather couch, she turned to me. "Why don't you enjoy your wine, Mallory?" She motioned to the seat. "I should introduce Cooper to a few people."

I felt somewhat protective over Cooper having to roam the room and tell half-truths, but I was well aware that this was Cooper's world and not mine. He squeezed my hand and met my eyes to see if this was okay with me. I nodded and dropped down onto the couch with my champagne.

It only took five minutes to get my bearings in the room full of more than a hundred publishing professionals. At first, I'd followed Cooper's progress around the groupings of people as Monia introduced him and they all nodded with big, practiced smiles. I wondered how many of them were telling half-truths or complete lies right back to him.

Soon, my attention drifted. Aside from those getting fawned over, or those doing the fawning, there were at least a dozen other loners like me—stray men and women stuck along a side wall, or at the bar, or in a lone armchair. These were clearly the unimportant-yet-supportive spouses. However, I was the only loner who conspicuously had an entire couch to myself.

I stood with my glass and meandered toward the nearest loner woman, who leaned against the wall, sipping what looked like a cup of coffee.

"Hi, I'm Mallory," I said, extending my hand. "Are you another of the author's wives? Should we form a club?" I chuckled at my own silly joke.

She smiled and shook my hand. "Anilee Marsh. And, no, I believe I'd have to form an *Editor's* Wives' Club." Now she chuckled, too. She placed her coffee down and picked up a cocktail plate from the ledge beside her. It contained a few veggies and a quiche. She reached for the quiche, took a bite, and grimaced a second later.

"Watery?" I asked. That was usually the biggest pitfall with quiche. "I always cook the veggies ahead before they go into the custard, and then blind-bake the crust to get a nice crisp on it."

She raised her eyebrows at me. "You know a thing or two about quiche."

My face warmed. "I go to culinary school." I still felt like some kind of chef-fraud every time I said it. "And I work in the evenings at this little bistro in Fox Hills, Pennsylvania. On weekends, I make their quiche." To get the focus off me, I went on with, "So do you get to come to a lot of these types of functions?"

Anilee was a tall slim woman in her fifties who looked a little underdressed in her dark gray pants and royal blue blouse. But glancing around once more, I realized not everyone was dressed up. Perhaps the more seasoned goers who attended these functions didn't bother.

"Get to...? Have to...?" She laughed. "About a million of them.

First time for you, I assume? Which one is your husband?"

I pointed across the room to where Cooper was surrounded by a group of five men with white hair. Monia stood nearby with a furrowed brow, typing into her phone. "In the checkered pants," I told Anilee.

She nodded. "Well, he's a looker, isn't he?" I giggled at the compliment. "He's talking to the editor-in-chief, Bill Haynes. My husband says Bill's a real bear, but look at him laughing now. Your man must have a sense of humor."

"He does," I agreed. "So your husband makes you come and stand by yourself all the time at these things?" I asked her seriously. Would I be asked to drive two and a half hours each way on a regular basis to stand by myself?

But who was I kidding? I wouldn't let Cooper go without me.

Anilee tilted her head, like she wasn't all that bothered. "I learn a lot about the business by hanging around.

It's not so bad, and then Harry and I have things to talk about when we get home. After twenty years of marriage, it's good to have a conversation starter." She smiled.

I wondered if Cooper and I would need conversation starters in twenty years. But I was stuck on her knowing a lot about this business.

"So let me ask you something. Have you ever heard of an author dealing with identity theft? Someone posing as them online?"

Anilee laughed like this was a very comical joke. I waited until she calmed down and saw that I was serious. "Oh, honey, that happens all the time! If your husband only has one person pretending to be him online, you just wait."

I felt a wave of relief. Clearly, this was why Cooper wasn't as bothered about it as I was. I still disliked people pretending to be someone they weren't. "It'll get worse?"

She nodded confidently. "Oh, yes. I've heard a thousand stories about authors chasing around imitators online to try and get them to stop."

"If other authors have been chasing around imitators for years, though, some of them must have had some success?"

She shrugged. "You could certainly hire an entertainment lawyer if you're worried about the principal of the thing, but I can't see it being worth the effort."

"This guy, whoever he is, he's charging money for access to some secret chapters, though. I signed up under my sister's name just to see what it was, and it's such bad writing." I was exaggerating how awful they were. Cooper hadn't felt the author in question was quite as unskilled, so I was likely biased.

"Oh, wow. I've never heard of that," Anilee told me.

"Would you know where to find a good entertainment lawyer?"

"I'm sure Harry does. I can ask him if you'd like?" She waved to someone across the room.

Did I want her to go to the trouble? Could Cooper and I afford an entertainment lawyer, and would I have to trek back and forth to Manhattan to meet with him?

Caught up in my warring thoughts, at first I didn't notice the man in a dark gray suit with salt and pepper hair sidled up beside Anilee. "Honey, they want our picture with the rest of the editing team."

"I'll get back to you." She winked at me. Harry slid an arm around her, and as he whisked her away, she added, "Don't worry, the photographers will be coming for you soon, too. These are big 'family' events, after all." She chuckled and let her husband lead her to the far wall of the room where editors had gathered with their spouses and a photographer waited.

I thought about introducing myself to another loner, so as not to be left on my own again, but just then, Cooper and Monia made their way back over to me.

"You should have let me tell my sailor joke," Cooper was saying.

"It wasn't good timing," Monia replied.

Cooper raised an eyebrow, clearly not agreeing, but I had a one-track mind about the Cooper Beck imitator.

"Monia, do you happen to know anything about entertainment lawyers?" I asked.

"Right, that," Monia said, turning to me with a sigh. "Listen, let me give you some advice, Mallory? Imitation is the highest form of flattery. Let this guy do his thing. It doesn't always matter what they're saying about you, as long as they're talking about you."

This was the sort of statement that made me bristle toward Monia. My husband had a good name. Or at least he had up until now. "Make sure Cooper regularly posts a note letting his fans know that his account is the only official one and that they shouldn't bother with any other accounts. It's all you can really do." She put a hand on my shoulder, an obvious attempt at trying to soothe me, but the motion was all wrong on her.

And then, in an instant, she flipped to another topic. Just like Monia.

I'd been telling Cooper he should get a better agent, one who actually had time to look out for his best interests. Still being in school, though, and new to the publishing biz, he seemed to carry a hyped-up nervousness when it came to literary agents. Cooper's former roommate, Pete, as well as any other creative writing students we'd had over for dinner, talked about literary agents like they were some kind of higher being—puppeteers of their lowly authors' very existence. I'd been trying to convince Cooper for the last year that he should have some clout by now. His agent should be working *for him*, and not the other way around, especially now that he was a bestselling author.

However, I sensed in the middle of this Christmas party wasn't the time to push this issue. Maybe Anilee would get me some good information about entertainment lawyers.

But I had one more quick question to ask, and if Cooper wasn't going to hound her for an answer, tonight might be my only chance. "I wanted to at least get his accounts verified. Some of the platforms require proof from companies collaborating with a public person of interest, so I'd just need a letter from you."

Monia responded with a half-nod, but her attention was on her phone, and her only answer was, "I have to take this," before she moved away from us to answer.

I held out an open hand to Cooper. Couldn't he see how rude and unhelpful she was? But Cooper only nibbled his lip and said, "Monia's being really strange tonight."

I tilted my head. "Strange? How so?" Monia had moved more than ten feet away, but I still lowered my voice so it could barely be heard over the top forty music.

Cooper shook his head. "She's asking me weird questions, like if we're planning to have kids soon, and where we're planning to relocate after school."

This seemed to me that Monia was taking a human interest in one of her clients for once. Then again, most of what Monia did was only for show.

"Was this in front of editors and publishing bigwigs?"

He shook his head again. "When it was just us. The thing is, she didn't seem to be asking in that casual way, like when you chat about life with a friend. She was asking like it was a big business discussion, and she kept making notes on her phone. Plus, she's been slipping away constantly to take phone calls and texts, like she's too busy for my publishing team."

"Hmm. You'd think she'd try to put her best foot forward when introducing you to these people."

"Yeah, that's what I thought," he said. "She just seems secretive and...different." Cooper snapped his mouth shut when Monia reappeared at our sides.

She pointed to where the editors had disbanded and said, "It's a good time to go get a photo, while it's not busy over there. They'll put it up on their website."

Like obedient puppies, Cooper and I nodded and moved over to the wall that had been draped with a black backdrop with their publishing logo, a large lit Christmas tree off to one side, and red carpet on the floor for photos.

But all I could think of was Monia and her strangeness tonight. If even Cooper had picked up on it, it clearly wasn't a matter of me being overly suspicious. Why would she be so interested in his personal life all of a sudden? What was so important on her phone that she couldn't stick to a conversation with an editor-in-chief for five minutes? And why didn't she seem to even want to help get Cooper's social media accounts verified?

I thought again of the photo and video clip on the imposter's website, the ones I'd never seen before. Did this imposter have other personal information on Cooper they were planning to share after the Christmas novel was finished?

I forced a smile for our photo, but I felt anything but happy. When Monia left us again for her phone, and Cooper's editor joined us for a photo, I kept my eyes peeled for Anilee or her husband, Harry, but I didn't see them anywhere.

In fact, for the next hour, I kept looking, but the only time I saw them, they were mixing with a large group of other professionals. After that, they disappeared again.

And ever since my conversation with Monia, she seemed to avoid us for the rest of the evening.

I pasted on a smile and did my part and decided that maybe tonight I should just have fun and enjoy Cooper's big first night at a publishing function.

Tomorrow, I would push to get the mystery of Cooper's imitator solved, even if it did turn out to be someone we thought was on our side.

SEVEN DAYS BEFORE

Christmas

THE NEXT MORNING, COOPER went to school early. I didn't have a class until this afternoon, followed by my shift at Baby Bistro.

I yawned as I trudged toward the coffee maker. Cooper and I had argued most of the drive home. It hadn't started out as an argument. He'd been letting out his frustrations about how Monia didn't seem to want to let him talk to any of the publishing executives for any length of time.

"It's like she has something to hide," he'd said.

And that's when I'd pounced. I'd told him how I'd never trusted Monia, and maybe she was responsible for the imposter on social media and the website that was making money off his good name.

He'd told me I was jumping to conclusions, and that Monia would never stoop to that level, but I disagreed. Monia definitely had a sneaky side, and I couldn't just think the best of every single person, the way Cooper seemed to be able to.

"Why won't you even consider looking for a new agent?" I'd asked.

"You don't understand. It isn't that easy, especially in the middle of my series."

"But what do you think she's hiding, Cooper?" I'd asked, figuring if I kept pushing, maybe he'd eventually come to the same conclusion: that perhaps Monia was the one hawking someone's unpublished work online through a slew of *@CooperBeck* handles.

But we'd just gone around and around the same mountain, and it seemed the more shade I threw in Monia's direction, the more he seemed to want to protect her.

"Don't you think it's at least worth looking deeper into this imposter?"

I'd finally gotten him to agree to that much, even with Monia's discouragement, and so I'd gotten up earlier than I wanted to track down an entertainment lawyer and at least figure out what kind of cost we'd be looking at. I dialed our oven to 350 for my favorite lemon-blueberry muffins, and then set up my laptop at our small kitchen table. I took a sip of my coffee and brought up my browser.

However, when I googled entertainment lawyers, my screen flooded with a million options, most of them in New York City or Los Angeles. I clicked on the first one listed in New York, but when the screen loaded to a close-up of a balding man that had a used-car-salesman gleam in his eye, I quickly backtracked to my search screen.

I let out a frustrated growl, which garnered Hunch's attention. He appeared in the kitchen doorway, surveyed the room, saw that Cooper wasn't anywhere in sight, and then sauntered off, his tail whipping back and forth.

Half an hour later, I had been to at least two dozen websites of entertainment lawyers, and all I'd discovered was that they all looked like shysters and they were all charging upward of $300 per hour.

I headed for the cupboards to gather my muffin ingredients, but when I passed the oven, I decided to check that the racks were near the middle. I pulled open the door, and it was completely cold.

I checked the dial on the oven, and it was still turned to 350. Our oven was an old model. In fact, in the first week we'd lived here, the door to it had come unhinged, and I'd had to spend a day making multiple trips to the hardware store to fix it. I reached inside, and the oven element was as cold as our chilly house.

Sighing, I placed the flour back in the cupboard and grabbed my phone from the table. After arguing all the way home last night, I didn't want to start today's conversation with a complaint, so I typed:

‹Morning Cooper. Listen, I'm sorry I was so indignant last night. I don't want to fight with you.›

A second later, Cooper's reply appeared.

‹I don't want to fight either Mal. If you think Monia's up to something, I'll look into it. And I think you're right to take the online imposter more seriously. Let me know what you think we should do.›

He followed it up with a heart emoji, which made me smile for the first time today.

‹Hey, I think the oven element is burned out. If you talk to Pete, can you ask him how hard that is to fix?›

Pete had been Cooper's former roommate at the university before Cooper had moved in with me. He had taken a leave from school to work at his dad's construction company and hoped to finish up his master's degree as soon as he had saved some more money. He hadn't been happy about it, but in general, Pete was skilled at fixing almost everything. He'd come to our rescue more than once since we'd moved into our house, repairing everything from leaky pipes to broken weather stripping. Cooper and I were both pretty much useless in that department, so it was good to have a friend like Pete, even if he no longer lived in Fox Hills. He still regularly came for dinner when he could, along with several others of Cooper's classmates.

‹Sure thing. What do you think of inviting him over for Christmas Eve?›

I sighed. I didn't want to go without an oven for a week. And besides that, Cooper and I had barely had any time off together since the summer. I had been hoping we could have a quiet Christmas, just the two of us.

But nevertheless, I typed:

‹Absolutely.›

Because if Cooper had such a big heart to want to be a friend to someone who'd had a tough year, I wasn't about to quell that instinct.

I looked down at my bathrobe, knowing I should really be dressed by this late in the morning. But now that I felt like I had Cooper's support, I'd thought of one more option.

I navigated to Cooper's publisher's website, picked up my

phone, and entered the number before I could chicken out. I'd already searched for Harry and Anilee Marsh in the phone book. There were far too many Marshes in the greater New York City vicinity, and so this was the only solution I'd come up with.

My armpits were moist with sweat, but I wasn't about to hang up. What if the publisher had caller ID? What if they recognized Cooper's home phone number?

There was no more time to fret about it as the receptionist answered my call and asked how she could help.

"May I please speak to Harry Marsh?"

I heard typing on the other end of the line. Then, "May I tell him who's calling?"

"Um, Mallory Beck." I said my name super fast, as though maybe she'd get it wrong, or no one would recognize me in any relation to Cooper, and somehow it would be this receptionist's fault and not mine for bothering a big-wig editor at work.

She put me on hold, and about three seconds later, the line clicked on with a male voice. "Harry Marsh here?"

"Hi, Mr. Marsh." I gripped my coffee cup hard to steady my hands and voice, trying to keep up at least some semblance of professionalism. "I'm not sure if you remember me, but I met you last night at the Christmas party. I was speaking with your wife, and—"

"Right, right! She was chatting about you the whole way home."

"She was?" I asked. If Anilee had remembered to mention my interest in an entertainment lawyer, there either hadn't been any other good conversation topics from last night, or she, too, thought I should pursue this.

But then Harry said, "Yes, she couldn't stop talking about your quiche recipe. She wanted to catch you before we left, but I had to head home early last night for an overseas Zoom meeting."

Oh. She remembered me because of my knowledge of quiche. But, still, while I had him on the line... "Actually, I had asked her about where to find a reputable entertainment lawyer, and she said you might have some ideas." I wanted to add the word "cheap" but instead, I added, "Preferably in the Pennsylvania area, if there is such a thing."

"Well, sure," Harry said. I heard him typing into a computer. "They're everywhere. There's a good one in Lancaster, in fact. Let me just look up his number for you." I waited on the line, holding my breath to the sound of his typing. So far he didn't seem bothered that I'd simply called him out of the blue to ask this. "Is this about that social media stalker you were telling my wife about?"

"Yeah. Yes," I said. It didn't bode well that he remembered me for the quiche and not for my need for an entertainment lawyer, if he'd clearly heard about both.

"As I told Anilee, this sort of thing happens, especially with bestselling novelists. I think it'll cost you more than it's worth. You should have Cooper's agent look into it for you, but here's the number I have for Martin Lucas in Lancaster, if you decide to follow up on it yourself." I was certain he didn't have time for the lengthy conversation necessary to explain why Monia Chapman wouldn't be much help in this area. He rattled off a phone number, and I scribbled it down. Then he added, "And would you mind if I passed your number along to my wife? She'd love to talk to you about that quiche."

FIVE DAYS BEFORE

Christmas

THANKFULLY, ENTERTAINMENT LAWYERS, or at least the one I made an appointment with, offered free consultations. The drive to Lancaster was just over half an hour, so I made arrangements for my next day off to drop Cooper at the university before borrowing his car.

He knew full well of my plans and appreciated me taking the reins on it, as he had to get his book draft to his editor before Christmas if he planned to have any time to enjoy himself over the holidays. The traffic thickened as I drove into the city, but I had no trouble locating the office of Martin Lucas, Entertainment Lawyer, situated in a tall brick building right at the city center.

I looked up at the towering building, sucking in a breath. If I did decide to retain this lawyer, he most certainly wouldn't be cheap.

My appointment was at nine twenty-five. I didn't know if that meant it would be a five-minute consultation or a thirty-five-minute one.

I took the elevator to the eighteenth floor, looking over my notes one more time. I was generally a competent notetaker. Research for Cooper's mystery novels had taught me that the memory was a fallible thing and you could never have too many notes.

I had the elevator to myself for a couple of floors, but then men in dark suits boarded and stepped off again, all before I reached my floor. I looked down at my red turtleneck, jeans, and knee-high boots, wondering if my outfit was a bit too casual for a lawyer visit.

But then the elevator dinged, taking my attention. I took one more deep breath, stepped off, and strode toward the office of Martin Lucas LL.M.

His office was well marked with a gold nameplate, and when I opened the door, it led me into a cozy reception area with a loveseat and an armchair, as well as a large mahogany desk where a receptionist sat.

I walked straight for the receptionist, but she wore a headset and nodded down at her desk as though she had someone on the line. I didn't interrupt, and after a few seconds, she said, "Right. And I'll get back to you with that before Tuesday."

She didn't say goodbye, so I wasn't sure she was done, even when she looked up at me and said, "Yes?"

"Oh!" I said after a lot of silent staring. "I have an appointment with Mr. Lucas at nine twenty-five?" Counselor Lucas? Or just Mr. Lucas?

Whatever the case, the lady didn't correct me. She had to be in her late fifties, but her dyed strawberry-blonde bob would have suited someone younger. She glanced at her computer screen and then back at me. "Sure. Take a seat." She motioned to the loveseat. "Mr. Lucas will be with you shortly."

Right. *Mr.* Lucas. I thanked her and sat on the edge of the loveseat, tapping my toes. I'd never met with a lawyer before, and suddenly, I felt out of my depth. This was Cooper's battle, after all. What if the lawyer laughed in my face and asked me why I was so concerned if Cooper's agent and publisher weren't? What if he looked at me like I was crazy when I brought up my suspicions of Monia?

Thankfully, I didn't have long to stew about this. The bobbed-haired woman stood and said, "Mallory Beck? Mr. Lucas will see you now." She led me to the heavy oak door, knocked twice, and then opened it for me.

I walked through to greet a tall man with a long dark beard reminiscent of Abraham Lincoln. "Hi, Mr. Lucas. I'm Mallory Beck." I held out my hand to shake, but he was already sitting again, his eyes on the paperwork on his desk.

"Yes, and you wanted to speak to me regarding an identity theft infringement?"

I sat across from him, this time on the edge of a leather armchair. The roomy, minimally-decorated office was a complete contrast to the intimate waiting room. "That's right. My husband is a novelist—a bestselling novelist," I added. "And I believe someone is imitating him online."

Mr. Lucas looked me in the eye and nodded for several long seconds, taking this in. Or maybe he was waiting for more.

"This person is all over Twitter, Facebook, Instagram, Snapchat, and TikTok, and even though he's pretending to be my husband, my husband, his agent, and his publisher say they have nothing to do with it, don't even know who the guy is." My voice faltered on the word "agent." I wasn't quite ready to suggest to this lawyer that he investigate her to see if she might be behind the money-making impersonation, but I was close. "Until recently, my husband wasn't even on social media," I added.

Mr. Lucas smirked. "Not on social media at all? Really?"

This was the part he focused on? I was over his and everyone else's amazement at this fact. I had come here because there was a serious problem, not because I needed another person to tell me how ridiculously long it took Cooper to get his own social media presence.

"Yes, but what about this imitator? Isn't this a clear case of identity theft?"

Mr. Lucas let out a long, loud sigh. "Well, yes, in a sense, certainly..."

My hope deflated. I'd wasted my last day off before Christmas coming here, and for what?

"The thing is," he went on, "there's a good possibility this person *is* named Cooper Beck, or he's using it as his own pen name and has his own set of writing. It sounds as though it could be a common name."

I felt flustered, at least in part because I was so out of my element in a lawyer's office. I reached into my purse and retrieved my notebook, which I'd left open to my page of notes.

I blurted the first word my eyes landed on. "Videos! But the guy has videos and pictures of *my* Cooper Beck!

They're on TikTok! They're on Instagram! Sure, most of them are from interviews already on the Internet, but this guy, he's honest-to-goodness trying to pretend he *is* my husband."

I was sure this was going to sell Martin Lucas on the seriousness of the matter, but he only let out another loud sigh. "So he's reposting items?" He didn't leave me time to answer. "I can see why this might feel like a violation of privacy, Mrs. Beck, but I have to say, as a public person of interest, you might want to look at this as a form of flattery." There was that word again. The more I heard it, the more it aggravated me. Mr. Lucas started to stand. "Now if that's all I can do for you...?"

I guess the time allotment for a free consultation was five minutes, after all. My eyes frantically scanned my notes, hoping I hadn't truly wasted my day for this.

"But the signup page!" I said, the second my eyes skimmed across the words. Realizing quickly that he would have no idea what I was talking about, I babbled on to explain. "All of his social media leads to a sign-in page where he asks for nine ninety-five per month to read some secret Cooper Beck chapters—and they're not even good! He's making money off pretending to be my husband."

I knew it was only ten bucks, but who knew how many people he had scammed into signing up, and besides, it really *was* the principle of the thing.

Mr. Lucas lowered back into his chair. "Hmm, well, if we're talking about fraud as well, you might have something here."

"Really?" Surprise rang out in my voice like a Christmas chime. I felt like I was the only one who had truly cared about the imposter until this very moment. "What can we do? Can we get him to stop? Can we sue him?"

Mr. Lucas pressed his hands toward the floor. "Now, now. Unless you have boatloads of time and money to spend, I wouldn't get too excited. Even if we sued the guy, it's fairly likely he's not worth much. Often these scammer websites are run by young tech guys trying to game the system and make a quick buck, until they realize the money isn't that great. It's such a popular scam this time of year, we've even coined a name for it. We call it the *Holiday Hustle*. It can be hard to catch these guys before they disappear. It could be a lot of effort for nothing."

"Okay, but if we can find him, we can at least stop him, right?"

Mr. Lucas shrugged. "Again, it depends on how important it is to you."

"It's important," I said, even though a niggling in the back of my head reminded me that it didn't seem all that important to Harry and Anilee

Marsh, who knew the business a lot better than I did. "But I don't have boatloads of money to spend."

Mr. Lucas leaned back in his chair, hands behind his head, and said, "Listen, Mrs. Beck, can I give you a piece of advice?" I nodded, and he went on. "Find yourself a young techy friend, someone who knows his way around the Internet. Have them look into the backend of the website this guy has made and find the ISP. From there, you can try and investigate ownership. If you can come back to me with a name and address of the owner, I can help you with a formal cease and desist letter. That usually works and will run you a half hour of legal fees, about $175. If I have my office do the background work, you're probably looking at several billed hours. You're not going to make any money off the guy this way, but if we try to take him to court over it, generally, the law makes impersonating somebody online a misdemeanor or third-degree felony, punishable by fines and a very small amount of jail time at most, depending on the severity of the crime. If you sued, you'd have to prove indisputable damages to get any kind of compensation. You'd have to hope the settlement would be enough to pay your legal fees. It may not be."

I nodded, filled with consternation. *Was* this worth it?

"Now, if there's nothing else," Mr. Lucas said, standing again.

And I supposed there wasn't. Nothing else to do but go home and make a decision.

I sat in Cooper's car with my head against the steering wheel, feeling the full weight of my discouragement. Being in the culinary industry, I didn't have a lot of techy friends, and neither did Cooper. I looked up at the lawyer's office and then pulled out my phone, scrolling through all of the fake Cooper

Beck's accounts to see what was new. I did it mostly out of habit now. It was all so repetitive, it helped me think.

But then I got to TikTok and a short new video clip loaded. It was of Cooper goofing around at the basketball court. He spun a basketball on his finger, left it mid-air to do a little dance spin, and then caught it. Of course he was talented, like he was with most things, but that wasn't what caught my attention. This was taken at the basketball court *near our house*.

The frame of the video was off to the side and kept getting obstructed by a tree, so I doubted Cooper knew he was being filmed.

I sucked in a breath. This imitator was way too close to our home for my comfort. My mind shot back to the student, Rudy Miller, who'd been kicked out of the university's creative writing program for stalking people on campus a few months ago, and the kitchen gadget that had too-coincidentally shown up in our new home's mailbox, unbidden, not long before that.

Was it possible Rudy Miller hadn't given up when he'd been kicked out of university? Maybe he was still stalking Cooper, but this time, he was playing around with his reputation online.

I shuddered, placing my phone into its holster, and started the car. I had just driven onto the freeway back toward Fox Hills when my phone started to play its musical ringtone. I glanced down, figuring it would be Cooper, but the screen said UNKNOWN CALLER.

Curiosity got the best of me, and I hit the Bluetooth answer button on Cooper's steering wheel. "Hello?"

"Hi, Mallory? It's Anilee Marsh. My husband gave me your number. I hope you don't mind."

"Oh, not at all!" I told her. "I was actually just meeting with an entertainment lawyer in Lancaster—one your husband put me in touch with."

"Well, Harry would certainly know who's good. Any promising news there?"

I shook my head, even though she wouldn't be able to see it. "Not really. He told me if I found someone technologically knowledgeable to get into the backend of the website and find this guy's address, he could charge me an arm and a leg to send a cease and desist letter."

"Hmm. Yes, lawyers certainly don't come cheap, do they?"

"But then just now I saw another video posted on this imitator's TikTok account. It's a video I've never seen of Cooper, and it looked like it was sneakily taken at the basketball court near our house."

"Near your house? Ugh, that is upsetting," Anilee said. I was glad I wasn't alone in thinking this. "You don't know anyone at your culinary school who might know about computers?" Culinary types were mostly artistic, not techy, but I mentally considered each of my classmates as I stared at the straight road in front of me. Then Anilee added, "Or at your bistro?"

And that's when my brain lit up. I hadn't known Rory, the other prep cook, long, and most of the time I did my best to focus on my own work, as I didn't want to get lumped in with her unwillingness to wear a hairnet or to follow other specific directions. But I did recall two things about her: She had just graduated high school, and her boyfriend, James, created websites for people in his spare time.

"Hang on. Maybe I thought of someone," I told Anilee. After explaining my connection and how I'd be seeing Rory the next night at work, I'd almost completely forgotten about the real reason for Anilee's phone call.

"So about that quiche recipe..." she said.

"Right!" I rattled off my email address and told her if she sent me her address, I'd email her the instructions from my culinary school recipe book the minute I got home. "And thanks for your help," I told her.

"I really didn't do anything, but you know, if you really think this guy's hanging around your town, it might be worth mentioning to the police."

Fox Hills was a small university town, mostly made up of students and teachers. It barely had a police department, or so I'd heard. But Anilee might be right. As far as I was concerned, this imposter of my husband's was too close for comfort.

"Hey, what do you know about Monia Chapman?" I asked on a whim. Anilee seemed to know a lot about the publishing professionals who attended parties regularly, and even if I was way off in my speculations, I doubted she'd do more than have a good chuckle. Even though Monia lived in Bayonne, New Jersey, a good distance too far for her to have traveled to our small town to film some basketball tricks, her secrecy and half-truths still bothered me.

"The agent?" Anilee asked. "She's well-known in the industry. A bit hard-nosed from what I've heard, but has some great clients."

"Do you think she's...trustworthy?" I asked.

"As far as I know," Anilee said lightly. But then her tone darkened. "Wait, you don't think—?"

"I don't know what to think," I quickly put in. I certainly didn't want to spread rumors about Monia within the publishing industry, at least until I had some solid proof that she might have been involved. "She was acting weird at the party the other night, though. Asking Cooper strange, personal questions, and acting really secretive."

"Let me do some poking around," Anilee said.

"Can you do it quietly?" I asked. "I don't want it to get back to her."

"You can count on my discretion," Anilee said. "I know she has family in Pennsylvania," she added, as if I'd mentioned my need for proof aloud.

After promising she'd get back to me if she found out anything, I thanked her and hung up.

At least I was no longer alone on my investigative team.

The police, as expected, weren't going to be of much help. Without a name or any ideas about where this imposter might be located, our local department didn't have the resources to launch a full investigation.

By the time I got home, just after lunch, Cooper was set up and busy working at the kitchen table. He usually only did that when I wasn't home. He must have gotten dropped off by another student.

"How'd it go?" he asked, slapping the lid of his laptop shut so hard, I worried it might break. I furrowed my brow, wondering if there was yet another member on my investigative team who didn't want me to see what he'd been researching.

But if Cooper were looking into the imposter or Monia, why wouldn't he just tell me?

Unless he'd found something he thought might upset me.

I hesitated in the doorway to the kitchen, but finally decided that if I were upfront about what I'd discovered, he'd see he could be, too. "The lawyer gave me a couple of things to think about," I told him. "But we can talk about it when you're done if you need to write." I motioned to his laptop.

Cooper smiled and pushed his laptop a few inches forward. He patted the chair beside him. "Tell me now."

I sat and helped myself to one of the zucchini muffins I'd brought home from class Wednesday. Cooper took one as well. I decided to start with the TikTok video, as that was new information that wouldn't cost us anything.

I pulled up the clip on my phone and turned it so Cooper could see. He studied the video for several seconds. His eyes flitted to the profile photo in the circle at the bottom. He clicked on it, and when all that came up was his own name, he clicked back. After several more long seconds of studying it, he said, "This was Sunday night."

"This last Sunday?" I asked. Now it really felt too close for comfort.

He nodded. "Nate lent me that jacket out of his car. Mine was thin and wasn't doing much to fight the weather." Nate was another guy in the creative writing program. Snow lined the perimeter of the court, but it had been shoveled away from the play area.

"Was it just you and Nate?" I asked.

He shook his head. "A group of us from school decided to meet up. Pete had the day off and had stopped by, so it was a spur of the moment thing." Cooper furrowed his brow at the video. I had been at Baby Bistro all last Sunday. "Maybe one of them took this?"

"Maybe..." I said. "But would they post it online as you after what happened with Rudy Miller?" Besides, the creative writing guys had become a tight-knit group. I couldn't see any of them doing this to Cooper.

"You're right. Not a chance."

As the video continued to loop, I pointed to the trees that kept obscuring the view of him. "To me, it looks like someone was filming this in secret."

"Yeah, I think so. We weren't paying much attention to passersby."

"Do you think this could be Rudy Miller again?" I asked.

He shrugged. "I never heard what happened to him after he left school. I'll ask around, see if anyone knows if he's still in town." He heaved out a breath. "And the lawyer, how did that go?" He rubbed my knee.

"He told me if I can find someone to get into the backend of the website and find out this guy's name and address, we could pay him a hundred and seventy-five dollars to send a letter on our behalf in hopes that he stops." My voice leaked out the hopelessness I felt about this dead-end.

But Cooper took my hand on top of the table. "Mal, if this guy's lurking around our town here, and if it would make you feel better to do something about him, I say a hundred and seventy-five bucks is worth your peace of mind."

"Really?" I asked.

He squeezed my hand. "Absolutely."

FOUR DAYS BEFORE

Christmas

COOPER LEFT BEFORE I was up the next morning, and it was only after he was gone and I traipsed into the kitchen that I realized he had never told me what he'd discovered on his laptop the day before. Surely, he must know he could trust me with whatever it was.

As I locked the front door, ready to head for Baby Bistro, our neighbor, Mrs. Brayman, called out to me. "Mallory, can I speak to you for a moment?"

I checked the time on my phone. I didn't want to miss the bus. Taking quick steps, I met her halfway across our small patch of snowy front lawn.

Mrs. Brayman, a stocky woman in her sixties, taught in the history department at the university. Both she and her husband were academic professors who intimidated me every time I'd had a conversation with them.

"Happy holidays, dear," she said as we met up.

"You, too," I said. All creativity for conversation went out the window when the Braymans were around.

"I just wanted to let you know that I'd seen a man coming from around behind your house the other day. I wondered if you might be having some repairs done?"

My heart stopped. "In our yard? Are you sure?" The second it was out of my mouth, I realized she wouldn't have gotten this wrong. But for once, I didn't care at all how stupid my nonsensical questions looked to Mrs. Brayman.

"We haven't hired any repairmen. Can you tell me what this guy looked like?"

There was a fence between our back and front yards, with a gate, but we never used it. Our backyard was even smaller than the front. In fact, I didn't think we'd used our back door since we'd moved in over six months ago.

Mrs. Brayman went on to describe a man with bushy gray hair and a limp. He had worn a big black parka, but she thought him quite frail underneath it. "I think he was driving a black sedan."

"And you didn't know who he was?" I asked. Our university town mostly consisted of familiar faces. I'd have to ask Cooper how old Rudy Miller was, and if he had a limp.

When she said no, I thanked her and raced back to our house to check the back door. Thankfully, it was locked. In fact, it took some force with my shoulder to get it open since it hadn't been used in such a long time.

In the backyard, there didn't seem to be any signs of trespassing. I triple-checked the lock and then raced through the house, out the front door, and to my bus stop.

Once on the bus, I texted Cooper.

‹Mrs. Brayman said some guy with gray hair and a limp was lurking around our backyard yesterday. What does Rudy Miller look like?›

Three dots appeared, and then:

‹Not like that. He's our age. No limp.›

I wasn't sure if that made me feel better or worse. A second later, he added:

‹But I asked Nate about Rudy. Apparently he moved back with his parents in Rochester.›

Rochester was a long way to come to sneak videos of unsuspecting authors. Then again, Rudy had lived here for several years. He could be staying with a friend.

But even I knew I was reaching now. The next questions that distracted me for the rest of my bus rider were about Monia Chapman, and if any of her male relatives might walk with a limp.

Before I knew it, I was at my stop. I rushed off the bus and in through the front doors of Baby Bistro, thankfully with five minutes to spare. I slipped out of my coat in our barely-used breakroom, and before I could head for the kitchen, Rory came in. She was usually scheduled at least an hour before opening, for cleaning and easy prep stuff, so she already had her apron on.

"Oh, hey! I wanted to talk to you," I said. "Your boyfriend creates websites, right?"

She looked me up and down and smacked her gum a couple of times before answering. "That's right."

"I need some help with something. Do you think he'd have any time?"

She didn't answer, but pulled her phone out of her apron pocket and her thumbs texted at a mile a minute.

Seconds later, she said, "After work tonight'll work. Here's his address. You can go by." She rattled off an address, and I typed it into my phone.

Thankfully, she didn't ask me what it was for. I didn't want to get into it with Rory if I didn't have to.

I was about to head for the kitchen when Rory said, "I think your husband was in earlier."

"In here?" I asked. "This morning, before opening?" She nodded. Cooper knew what time we opened, and I was pretty sure I'd told him what time I started today. "Are you sure it was him?" He came in every couple of weeks, often with a friend from class, or to write if he needed a change of scenery. My employee discount and the fact that he didn't have to make his own food at home usually made the trip worth it for him.

Rory shrugged. "I don't know anyone else who wears bright green pants."

Cooper did have a memorable wardrobe. "And you told him I wasn't here yet?" I wondered why Cooper hadn't mentioned coming by in his texts.

Rory grabbed her lip balm from her coat and led the way back to the kitchen. "I didn't talk to him. I think he just talked to Chef Paul."

I nodded and got to work as soon as we stepped into the kitchen. Cooper had a lot on his mind these days between his school project and the deadline for his novel. It shouldn't surprise me that he'd stopped by at the wrong time and then neglected to mention it.

I went to where James lived at his parents' house straight from work.

The guy with unwashed shoulder-length dark hair who answered the door looked a little on the greasy side for Rory. But if he had the brains I was after, who was I to judge?

"James?" I asked.

He opened the door wider. "Rory said you need a website?"

I followed him inside and slipped out of my boots. From there, he led the way to a dining room, where his desktop computer, along with all of its components, took up most of the table. Someone was making noise in the kitchen, but whoever it was didn't bother us.

"Well, not exactly," I said, taking the chair beside him. "Actually, I'm wondering if you can hack into an already-existing website."

His eyes widened and he whispered, "Shhh," before glancing over his shoulder toward the kitchen.

I figured I should at least calm his nerves. "Not 'hack' exactly," I said quietly. "I want to find the owner of a website. They're the ones who are doing something wrong, not me. Can you help with that?"

After a pause where James studied my eyes to see if I was genuine, he finally nodded. I passed him over a slip of paper, where I'd written the URL of the website that contained the fake Cooper Beck's Christmas story.

James's hands flew over his keyboard. It clack-clacked loudly in response. I watched his screen, but as lines upon lines of code appeared, I quickly realized I was way out of my depth. This was why I needed an expert—even a teenage one.

He kept clack-clacking. Watching James's face was more telling than watching the screen. His eyebrows would raise, and his eyes would light up...only a second later to dip and he'd shake his head. That happened a number of times before he said, "Ahhh, there you are," and clack-clacked through another half dozen screens quickly.

As he worked, he started to explain his process. "The guy had set it up under a fake company name containing a string of non-pronounceable numbers and letters." He pointed to it on the screen. It read: 712PK198. "I googled it," James continued, "and it doesn't lead anywhere."

"Could it be a license plate number or something?" I asked.

James shrugged. He pulled up a new browser window and pasted the numbers and letters into the search bar, along with the words "license plate." He skimmed screens and clicked through them too fast for me to read a single word. After less than a minute, he said, "Nope. Not a U.S. one for sure." He clicked back to his other browser window. "Anyway, that's not the important part. Who cares what fake company name he used, I've got his real name."

James hit one more solid click on his keyboard, and a new screen appeared. He pointed to two words I otherwise may not have recognized as a name: Pirro Klytaimnestra.

"That's the guy? That's him?" I asked, quickly pulling out my phone and taking a snapshot of the entire screen. I'd never heard the name, so I doubted he was part of the small creative writing department at the university.

James nodded. Then he clicked on another screen he had open. "It lists this as his address in the Whois database..." He noticed my confusion and added, "The database for contact info for any domain holders." I nodded, and he went on. "I looked up the address, and it lists a different person as the resident, so I dunno."

As he showed me each bit of new information, I snapped photos of them. I tried hard not to focus on the fact that the address in question was an apartment right here in Fox Hills, Pennsylvania. "So if he's not at that address, what do I do? Google his name?"

James shook his head. "Did that. Not much comes up for this guy, not even a Facebook profile, which tells me you're probably right. The guy's probably shady." My first instinct was to tell him my husband hadn't had a Facebook profile until very recently, and he wasn't shady, but thankfully I caught myself, knowing arguing wouldn't do us any good. I opened my mouth to ask again what I should do, but he answered my question before I could. "Your best bet is this Gmail address. People don't really delete Gmail addresses—there's never any need to. If you want to get a hold of the guy, that's how I'd do it."

"Okay, thanks a lot." I was a little deflated, but at the same time, I hoped the guy, Pirro, whoever he was, had moved on from Fox Hills, at least as his permanent residence. "And how much do I owe you?" I asked.

He shrugged like he was going to say, "Any friend of Rory's is a friend of mine." But what he actually came out with was, "Fifty bucks?"

I nibbled my lip. The truth was, Rory and I weren't friends, certainly not close ones, and for all the times I'd inwardly grumbled about her, I should probably pay the guy double.

Besides, I got what I came for.

After leaving James's parents' house, I headed straight back to our town's small police station. On the bus ride there, I googled Pirro Klytaimnestra and then added "Rudy Miller" to the search. When nothing came up, I tried the name "Chapman." James was right. This guy had almost no information listed about him on the web.

When I opened the glass door to the police station, the same officer manned the front desk again and seemed to recognize me instantly. His light blue police shirt stretched tight across his chest and stomach, and I wondered if he'd put on weight since joining the force. He had a nice smile, though, and had truly seemed disappointed that he couldn't help me the last time I'd been in.

"I'm not sure if this will help, but I've got the guy's name." After hearing about him sneaking around our yard, I thought a restraining order might be called for, or I hoped this cop could at least tell me if Pirro Klytaimnestra still lived in Fox Hills, Pennsylvania. I glanced down at his nametag, which read, "RHODES."

I explained the trespassing and showed him the name. He typed it into a computer on the front desk. After a few seconds of scrolling and looking at the screen, he told me, "The guy doesn't have any prior infractions here in Fox Hills, or even within the state."

"No?" I asked, prodding, hoping he could tell me more.

But he only said, "I'm afraid that's all I can help you with, ma'am. Do let us know if he approaches either you or your husband in person with any kind of threat, but your best bet is to find a lawyer and come against him that way."

Right, so I was back to the big bucks.

I stewed about it all night. Cooper had a writing group and I had homework, but none of it was enough to take my mind off my questions about Pirro Klytaimnestra. Did the guy still live in Fox Hills? Did he follow

Cooper around regularly? Had he ever followed me or lurked around our yard when I was home? Could he have been the one who had left me the can opener when we'd first moved in and not Rudy Miller?

But that was months ago. What were the chances this guy had just lain low until now?

TWO DAYS BEFORE

Christmas

MONDAY MORNING, I SKIPPED my first class, determined to check out the address James had uncovered for me. Even if Pirro Klytaimnestra was no longer listed as living there, maybe he was using yet another alias. Or perhaps someone in the apartment building could tell me something about him.

Cooper was supposed to have had a meeting with his professor, but he ducked out of it, feigning sickness, as he wasn't about to let me go to this imposter's apartment alone.

Besides, the apartment complex wasn't far. In Fox Hills, everything circled the university grounds. We took Cooper's car and arrived within minutes. Someone was leaving the building as we arrived and held the glass door open for us. What luck!

But then we climbed to the third floor, knocked on the door, held our breath, and...no answer.

Cooper and I traipsed back down the stairs, but before leaving, I ran a finger along the listings beside the front door. There was no Pirro Klytaimnestra listed, and apartment 302 listed a G. Harmon, which I made a note of. The MANAGER was listed in 101. Without thinking twice, I pressed that button.

A second later, a gravelly voice came on the line. "Yup?"

"Hi there," I said. "Can we come in and talk to you for a second?"

A sigh and a pause. And then a buzzer.

We pulled open the door and navigated to apartment 101, located right beside the small lobby.

As the unshaven fortysomething man in a dirty T-shirt pulled the door open, I launched into my spiel. This was our last hope at finding the imposter in person.

"Hi there, we're looking for a guy named Pirro Klytaimnestra in 302?" I stumbled over the name I'd never said aloud before. "This is the address we have for him, but no one answered at his door. I wondered if he still lives here?"

The man looked over Cooper, from his dark curly hair to the bright green pants he'd worn again. Then he huffed out a sigh, left his door wide open without inviting us inside, and moved into his apartment. I didn't particularly want an invitation inside, as it looked and smelled like his last dozen dinners hadn't been cleaned up from the front room. He disappeared from view, and I only hoped he was in there checking the name for us. I looked at Cooper. He held out his hands and shrugged. At least I wasn't the only one left clueless here.

A minute later, the man returned, scratching his neck. I tried not to think about whether there might be fleas or bedbugs inside his apartment. "Nope. Not here no more."

"No?" I prodded for more.

He shook his head. "S'fars I can remember, guy's a drifter. He only lived here a few months. A couple's in that place now."

"Did he have gray hair? Or a limp?" I asked.

The guy raised an eyebrow, like he thought I was crazy. "Guy couldn't have been twenty-five. Blond. No limp that I saw."

"And he didn't leave you a forwarding address?" There was my sleuthing husband, finally kicking in with a good question.

But the answer was no. No forwarding address. No Pirro Klytaimnestra.

Cooper went straight to the university from there to see if he could catch his meeting after all, but I headed home.

As soon as I walked in the front door, my cell phone rang. I'd logged Anilee Marsh's name into my phone, so it came up across the screen.

I swiped to answer as I slipped out of my boots and headed for the living room. "Hello?"

"Hi, Mallory. Anilee here. Listen, I asked around quietly about Monia Chapman and found out something very interesting."

I dropped onto the left-hand side of our couch. Hunch was curled up on the right, but he opened an eye, saw me there, and then stretched and scampered off. It was never fun feeling like a disappointment to someone in your household every time you came

134

home, even if it was only a cat. But I had more important things on my mind.

"Interesting how?" I asked.

"Well, let me ask you this. Did you know Monia was retiring next week?"

My eyes went wide. "Retiring? Are you sure?" She hadn't said a word about it to Cooper. In fact, he regularly used the words "next month" and "next year" when talking about his agent. She must've known at the Christmas party, and she looked us straight in the eye and didn't say a word.

"Apparently, she's been pretty quiet about it, trying to secure a couple of deals before she leaves."

"Before she leaves and just drops all of her clients, high and dry," I added.

Anilee sighed. "I'm sorry not to have better news, Mallory. If Harry or I can help your husband connect with a new agent, do let us know."

I thanked her and said goodbye, already dreading having to pass this information along to Cooper, and right before Christmas, too. I'd sent Anilee my quiche recipe, but I'd send her my lemon-blueberry muffin recipe as well to thank her and to apologize for being so short with her on the phone. Someone with a working oven might as well enjoy those yummy muffins.

Next, I navigated to Martin Lucas's phone number on my cell. His receptionist picked up, and when I said I only had one quick question, I talked her into putting me through to her lawyer boss.

"Martin Lucas," he answered.

"Hi there, it's Mallory Beck. I promise I won't take up too much of your time, but I had one quick question. Can we take care of that cease and desist letter through an email?"

His answer was yes.

At least one thing had gone right today, but in that moment, Cooper and I became $175 poorer.

THE DAY BEFORE
Christmas

ON CHRISTMAS EVE, neither Cooper nor I felt much like celebrating. Cooper had worked hard, though, even through his despondency, and gotten his draft into his publisher, so at least we had a little time to wallow together.

I'd bought some ingredients to make my special Holiday Minestrone for Cooper to try, but I wasn't even feeling motivated to cook. The one thing I was thankful for was that Pete had texted Cooper this morning to let him know he wasn't going to be able to make it for dinner tonight, after all. As much as I wanted my oven fixed, I didn't have it in me to entertain, and I doubted Cooper did either.

We sat on the couch together, leaning into one another. I had my feet curled up beside me, while Cooper had his furry friend curled up beside him. We sat together, staring at the multi-colored lights on our Christmas tree. Cooper had wanted to string popcorn to decorate, like he had as a kid. I preferred forgetting my childhood Christmases, so I'd been happy to comply a month ago when we put the tree up. This wasn't the perfect Christmas I'd hoped for, but at least we were together and our house looked festive.

"Well, there's one good thing about this Christmas," Cooper said.

"What's that?" I snuggled my head into his shoulder, more than ready to hear about this "one good thing," whatever it was.

"I'm pretty sure you're going to like your gift." I could hear the smirk in his voice, but it only reminded me that I had absolutely nothing under the tree for Cooper. I'd put all my hope into that book arriving in time and hadn't had time between school and work to rush out and buy anything else last-minute. "It should be here any time now," he added.

I opened my mouth to tell him I really didn't even want a gift, and how sorry I was that his hadn't arrived, and likely would never arrive, when our doorbell rang.

Cooper just sat there, scratching a finger under Hunch's neck.

"Aren't you going to get it?" I asked, sadness leaking out in my voice.

Cooper couldn't seem to fight his grin. He motioned to the door. "You go ahead."

I tried to keep my sigh inaudible as I pushed to my feet and plodded to the door. I opened it, and an elderly man with gray hair stood a few feet away on our porch. He wore a heavy parka, and hearing the door, he turned and moved toward me. He *limped* toward me.

My mouth went dry.

"Mrs. Beck?" he asked.

I nodded and forced out one word. "Pirro?"

He tilted his head at my question, confused. "No, it's Albert. Albert Rolly. Is your husband home, Mrs. Beck?"

That's when I noticed the item in his hands. A blue-and-black softcover book with the word "Breathless" taking up most of the cover. I looked from the book to his face and then back down at the book again.

That was when Cooper appeared over my shoulder. "Everything okay out here?" he asked. And then, it seemed, Cooper was at a loss for words, too.

"Merry Christmas," Mr. Rolly said, extending the book toward Cooper. "I believe this is for you. Your wife was very concerned that you received it before Christmas. I live nearby in York county. Kept stopping by, but there was never anyone home. Thought about leaving it out back, but I didn't know if you'd find it there."

I finally found my voice. "Mr. Rolly, thank you so much! I can't tell you how much this means to me. To us," I added, motioning between me and my still-speechless husband.

"Your wife tells me you're also a published author," Mr. Rolly said. "I'll have to pick up one of your books. Maybe it'll be my Christmas gift to myself." He laughed, seemingly very comfortable with fans who were too starstruck to speak to him.

"Hang on just one second," I said. I felt bad for leaving Cooper on his own to silently fan-boy with his idol, but not badly enough to stay. I raced back to Cooper's office and returned seconds later with an author copy of his latest published mystery. It had released in August. "Merry Christmas!" I said, passing it over.

He chuckled and took the book from me. Cooper still had a dozen author copies that neither of us had an idea what to do with. "It will be now," Mr. Rolly said.

"I—I love your work," Cooper finally got out. I'd never seen my husband this nervous, not once in the two years I'd known him, not even the first time he asked me out or leaned in to kiss me. But I was incredibly glad to be giving him this butterfly moment now.

"And I'm sure I'll love yours," Mr. Rolly said, holding up the hardcover book I'd just given him. "I really have to be going, but I'm so glad to have caught you at home on Christmas Eve. Y'all have a Merry Christmas now," he said, moving down our front steps with the help of the railing.

"You too, sir," Cooper said.

"And thank you so much!" we both added at the same time.

As he slipped into the driver's seat of his dark sedan, I smiled up at my husband. His cheeks were a warmer brown than I'd ever seen them.

"You..." he said, pulling me into him and kissing me on the forehead. "So sneaky." Apparently, he was still having trouble with full sentences. Albert Rolly's car disappeared around the block, and Cooper and I were about to move back inside when a large utility van pulled up along the curb, right in front of our house.

"Ah, perfect timing!" Cooper said. "And now for your Christmas gift."

I furrowed my brow, waiting for a delivery driver to hop out of the driver's seat and head up to our porch with a small box. But instead, two men emerged on either side of the cab and moved toward the rear of the truck. They slid up the large door, and a moment later had set up a ramp down to the road.

I looked at Cooper, confused. He was all grins as he placed his precious book on the side table inside the doorway and then hurried out to meet the men at the road. I watched from the door as the three of them wheeled a gigantic brown box with a red bow on the top from the truck, up our driveway, and onto our porch.

"What is it?" I said as Cooper and I moved inside and the two delivery men measured the doorway.

"You'll see," he said.

It didn't take them long to get it inside, but it wasn't until they wheeled it toward the kitchen that an idea of what it might be occurred to me.

"You got me a new oven?" I exclaimed, almost breathless with excitement.

We followed the delivery men into the kitchen, and by the time we got there, the box was falling away from the new appliance on all four sides.

"A double oven?" I couldn't help the shriek of excitement that left my mouth. "How can we afford this, Cooper?"

"My advance came in. I hope it's what you want," Cooper said, all grins. "I had to get some help from your boss on choosing one you'd like."

"That's why you went in to see Chef Paul when I wasn't there?" It was probably also why he'd slapped his laptop shut as soon as I walked in the room. I threw my arms around him. "It's perfect! I absolutely love it!" I punched him playfully on the arm. "Now who's sneaky?"

I stood staring at my beautiful new appliance for a long time while the skilled delivery and installation workers got busy removing our elderly broken-down oven and replaced it with a shiny new stainless steel double version. My mind raced with items I'd have to get on a last-minute shopping trip, so I could make Cooper a delectable Christmas dinner. It likely wouldn't be easy to come by a fresh turkey, but perhaps I'd get a turkey breast, some phyllo, and some cranberries, and come up with something fun and delicious.

His cell phone rang, but I couldn't look away from my beautiful new cooking apparatus until he said, "It's Monia," in a deadpan voice.

Leave it to Monia to call on Christmas Eve, and finally admit she was leaving her clients high and dry to retire. Cooper had been too busy to even start on the search for a new agent, and he'd been too embarrassed to let me contact the Marshes for help.

He headed for the living room to take the call. I had a hard time tearing myself away from my gleaming new gift, but I finally convinced myself that Cooper needed me more than my oven did right now.

By the time I made it to our living room, he was already nodding into his phone. "Yeah, I heard," he said, still deadpan. "It doesn't really matter who told me, does it?"

And then a pause where he listened and nodded, and I wondered how on earth Monia Chapman could have so little humanity that she'd drop a bomb like this on Christmas Eve.

But then the strangest occurrence: Something resembling a *smile* formed on Cooper's face. "You're kidding me," he said. "You're sure?" Another pause. "Okay, yeah, I can do that."

A second later, he hung up, looking almost as stunned as he had when Albert Rolly had shown up at our door.

"What?" I asked, wondering if I was reading him wrong. Maybe he wasn't happy. Maybe he was so depressed he'd taken on the crazed look of a half-wit.

But then he opened his mouth and said, "Mitch Reynolds." He must have seen my confusion because he added, "Monia convinced him to sign me. Mitch Reynolds," he said again, and when he noticed my lack of elation, he explained, "He's Albert Rolly's agent. He represents some of the best authors in the world."

"Yeah, he does," I said, a grin covering my face now, too.

"Monia wanted to get a few things in place before she announced her retirement, one of which was to get her clients connected with new agents. She convinced him I wouldn't be too busy raising a family to deliver three books in the next two years."

Now I felt bad for judging Monia so harshly.

Cooper grabbed me close and kissed me, this time on the lips. "It's the perfect Christmas, isn't it?"

Almost. I couldn't help the errant thought.   Our   embrace   was interrupted, but this time by a ding from my phone. I pulled away just enough to check it. I had a new email update from Martin Lucas's office:

Dear Mr. and Mrs. Beck,
We sent the cease and desist email, as requested, and received a response within half an hour. Because of all the legwork you'd done, it was very little work on our end. This one's on the house. Happy Holidays.
See below.
Yours,
Martin Lucas LL.M.

Dear Mr. Lucas,
I'm so sorry. I didn't mean to cause any trouble. It was just some fanfiction, and I didn't know it would bother anybody, but I'll take it down right away.
Pirro

Martin Lucas had been right. It sounded like some young kid—maybe or maybe not a true fan—who was trying to make a buck, perhaps without his parents finding out.

By that afternoon, I'd stocked up on groceries, and every single one of the fake Cooper Beck social media accounts had been deleted. The website with the sign-in page was gone, too. I'd probably never know how much he'd made off Cooper's name, but at least I was no longer concerned for our safety or the injustice of it.

Sure, I'd solved the crime, but this one never felt right.

Not seeing the remorse on Pirro's face or knowing he'd had any kind of slap on the wrist from doing it, the investigation never quite felt finished to me.

At least we'd figured all of it out, and just in time for Christmas. Our truly perfect Christmas. The only one we'd ever get.

I always wondered if I'd come across Pirro Klytaimnestra again. A year after Cooper was gone from my life, I still sometimes wondered when I might see the imposter again.

THE END

Start on the first of the full-length Mallory Beck Cozy Culinary Capers:

Murder at Mile Marker 18
A Mallory Beck Cozy Culinary Caper
(Book 1)

Perfect for fans of Molly Fitz and Christy Barritt.

An unlucky amateur sleuth, an adorable cop, and a cat with a hunch...

If anyone had told Mallory Beck she would become Honeysuckle Grove's next unschooled detective, she would have thought they were ten noodles short of a lasagna. Her late husband had been the mystery novelist with a penchant for the suspicious. She was born for the Crock-Pot, not the magnifying glass, and yet here she is, elbow-deep in fettuccine, cat treats, and teenagers with an attitude, the combination of which lands her smack-dab in the middle of a murder investigation.

Maybe she should have thought twice about delivering a casserole to a grieving family. Maybe she should have avoided the ever-changing green eyes of her seventh-grade crush—now the most heart-stopping cop in town. Maybe she should have stopped listening to the insightful mewls of her antagonistic cat, Hunch, who most likely wants *her* to be the town's next murder victim.

Whatever the case, Mallory Beck got herself into this investigation, and she has a distraught teenage girl counting on her to deliver the truth.

Buy Murder at Mile Marker 18 Now!

Would you do me a favor? Reviews are super powerful when it comes to getting attention for my books. They help bring them to the attention of other readers. If you enjoyed this book, I would be grateful if you would take just five minutes to leave an honest review on Amazon, GoodReads, and/or Book Bub. (It can be as short as a couple of sentences). Thank you!

Join My Cozy Mystery Readers Newsletter Today!

Sign up now, and you'll get access to a special epilogue to accompany this series—an exclusive bonus for newsletter subscribers. In addition, you'll be the first to hear about new releases and sales, and receive special excerpts and behind-the-scenes bonuses.

Go to the below link to sign up and receive your bonus epilogue:

https://BookHip.com/RPXZGR

Turn the page to find a recipe from
Mallory's Recipe Box...

Mallory's Cranberry-Feta Christmas Kale Salad

This crisp and delicious Cranberry-Feta Kale Salad has all the colors and flavors to make this the perfect Christmas salad recipe. A delicate trio of sweet, tangy lemon, and salty from the feta combines to create this deliciously healthy salad.

Kale doesn't wilt like lettuce, so you can assemble this salad up to a day in advance. (Just be sure to save the feta and the dressing to add at the last minute.)

Ingredients:

1 bunch of kale, washed, trimmed, and chopped (about 8 cups chopped)

½ cup dried cranberries

½ cup sliced almonds, chopped walnuts, or pecans

1 medium Honeycrisp apple, cored and sliced (or your favorite apple variety)

½ cup feta cheese crumbles

Lemon Vinaigrette:

⅓ cup olive oil

¼ cup fresh lemon juice (from about one lemon)

1 clove minced garlic

2 teaspoons Dijon mustard

½ teaspoon salt

⅛ teaspoon black pepper

Instructions:

Remove the tough stem from all the kale leaves by laying flat on a cutting board and slicing off with a sharp knife. Wash the kale leaves. Chop into bite-size pieces and remove excess water using a salad spinner or dry with paper towels. Add to a large bowl.

Add the cranberries, sliced or chopped nuts, sliced apple, and feta cheese crumbles.

To make the lemon vinaigrette, combine all vinaigrette ingredients in a bowl and whisk to combine. Pour vinaigrette over salad and toss gently to combine.

Let sit for ½ to 1 hour to allow the kale leaves to soften slightly. Spread onto a large serving platter and garnish with additional cranberries, feta, and sliced apples.

Enjoy!

Up next in the Mallory Beck Cozy Culinary Capers:

Murder at the Town Hall
A Mallory Beck Cozy Culinary Mystery (Book 3)

An eye witness to a murder, a crush-worthy cop who needs her help, and a cat with a hunch. What could possibly go wrong?

Mallory Beck isn't in the habit of involving herself in local politics, but when she supports a new friend at a Ministry of Education meeting and the main speaker is found dead on the steps of the Town Hall, she finds herself smack-dab in the middle of another murder investigation. Her cat, Hunch, who loves a good mystery, is thrilled, and as usual, helps her discover the first clue.

Mallory's clever friend and former preteen crush, Alex, is on the case. He's been recently promoted to detective within the Honeysuckle Grove Police Department, but when he's paired with a lackadaisical superior who continually botches investigations, Mallory and her famously delicious baking comes to the rescue.

After all, the easiest way to a suspect's truth might just be through their stomach.

Order Murder at the Town Hall now!

About the Author

Denise Jaden is a co-author of the Rosa Reed Mystery Series by Lee Strauss, the author of several critically-acclaimed young adult novels, as well as the author of several nonfiction books for writers, including the NaNoWriMo-popular guide Fast Fiction. Her new Mallory Beck Cozy Culinary Mystery Series will continue to launch throughout the year, and you can add the first book to your reading list on GoodReads right now. In her spare time, she homeschools her son (a budding filmmaker), acts in TV and movies, and dances with a Polynesian dance troupe. She lives just outside Vancouver, British Columbia, with her husband, son, and one very spoiled cat.

Sign up on Denise's website to receive bonus content as well as updates on her new Cozy Mystery Series. Find out more at www.denisejaden.com

Sign up on Denise's website to receive bonus content as well as updates on her new Cozy Mystery Series. Find out more at www.denisejaden.com

Also by Denise Jaden

The Mallory Beck Cozy Culinary Capers:

Book 1 – Murder at Mile Marker 18

Book 2 – Murder at the Church Picnic

Book 3 – Murder at the Town Hall

Christmas Novella – Mystery of the Holiday Hustle

Young Adult Fiction:

Losing Faith

Never Enough

Foreign Exchange

A Christmas Kerril

The Living Out Loud Series

Nonfiction for Writers:

Writing with a Heavy Heart

Story Sparks

Fast Fiction

Made in United States
Orlando, FL
05 December 2021

11175711R00104